Groundwood Books / Douglas & McIntyre
720 Bathurst Street, Suite 500
Toronto, Ontario M5S 2R4

Distributed in the USA by Publishers Group West
1700 Fourth Street
Berkeley, CA 94710

We acknowledge the financial support of the Canada Council for the Arts, the Ontario Arts Council and the Government of Canada through the Book Publishing Industry Development Program for our publishing activities.

National Library of Canada Cataloging in Publication Data
Popp, Monika
Farm year
A Groundwood book.
ISBN 0-88899-452-4
1. Farm life—Juvenile fiction. I. Title.
PS8581.066F37 2002 jC813'.6 C2001-903086-X
PZ7.P7963Fa 2002

Printed and bound in China by Everbest Printing Co. Ltd.

Farm Year

STORY AND PICTURES BY

Monika Popp

ADDITIONAL PICTURES BY

Regine Frick-von Schmuck

A Groundwood Book
Douglas & McIntyre
Toronto Vancouver Buffalo

To my family
Monika Popp
In memory
of my best friend, Monika
Regine Frick-von Schmuck

1 • A Calf is Born

IT was the end of August. The trees were already losing some of their leaves, and the hedges smelled of rosehips. The wheat stood pale gold in the fields, ready for cutting. In the mornings a thick mist lay over the ponds and meadows.

But the little calf knew nothing about any of this when she came into the world on a prairie farm one day. Her mother licked her brown-and-white skin until she stood up on wobbly legs and hungrily searched for the udder. It was all the newborn calf could manage just to open her eyes and drink until she was full. Then she lay down on the soft straw and fell asleep.

In the beginning the calf stayed in her stall, close to her mother's big rough tongue and udder full of rich milk. But childhood is short for a Holstein dairy calf. The farmers want to sell the mother's milk. So after two weeks, the small brown-and-white calf was taken from her mother, whose milk would be pumped through a machine from now on.

The little calf was herded into the back of a trailer with several other calves. The cattle trailer began to rumble down the highway. Dust streamed through the rails as the trailer picked up speed. The little calf cried piteously.

The truck stopped in front of a busy auction barn. Many other farmers were pulling into the lot with their cattle. The animals were unloaded and herded into the hall. Gates slammed open and shut, and the air was filled with loud voices and the sounds of bellowing animals.

The little calf was put in a crowded pen. A man placed a white card with a number on each calf. If the calf was a female, he drew a line under the number. But he forgot to do that for the brown-and-white calf, so she was put with a group of young bull calves by mistake.

There were many farmers in the auction hall, including Victor, from Big Bear Farm, and his ten-year-old son, Jan. They had a lot of good hay this year — more than their beef cattle could eat over the coming winter. They were looking for some half-grown steers to add to their herd, but so far they hadn't seen any.

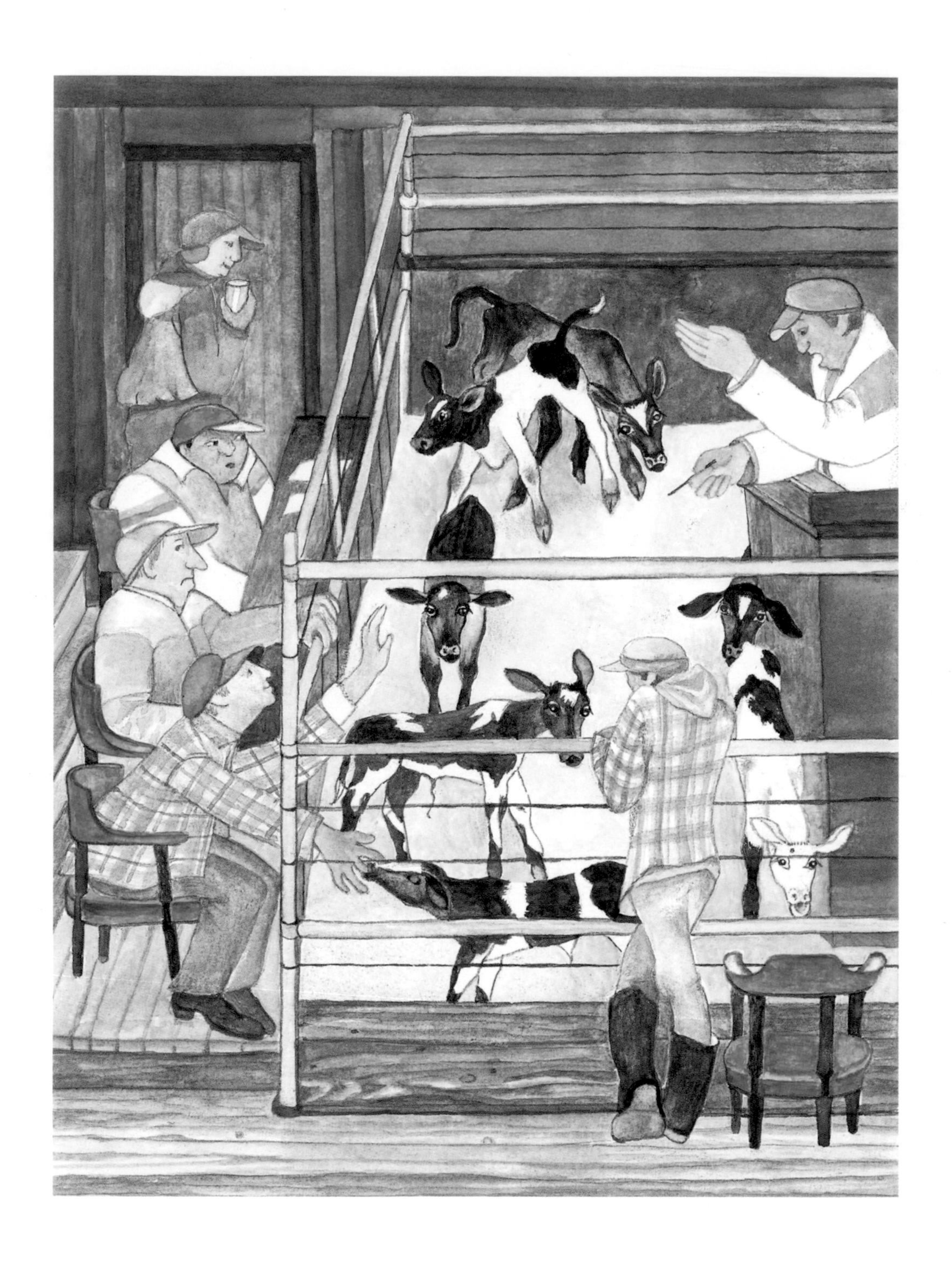

Now the man opened the gate and drove all the calves into the hall with a long pole. The strongest animals were sold immediately. At the end, only seven very small Holstein bull calves were left, including the brown-and-white one, number 63.

The auctioneer lowered the price again and again, but nobody wanted to buy the seven male Holsteins. Then Jan's father raised his hand.

"Are you going to take those little things?" asked Jan. "They're dairy calves. We run a beef farm."

"Going, going, gone!" cried the auctioneer, and he hammered on his block three times. He looked around at the crowd to see who had made the bid.

"And the seven steers go to ... "

"Victor Sullivan!" called Jan's father.

"To Victor Sullivan."

"Great!" shouted Jan, leaping for joy. "They'll be happy with us!"

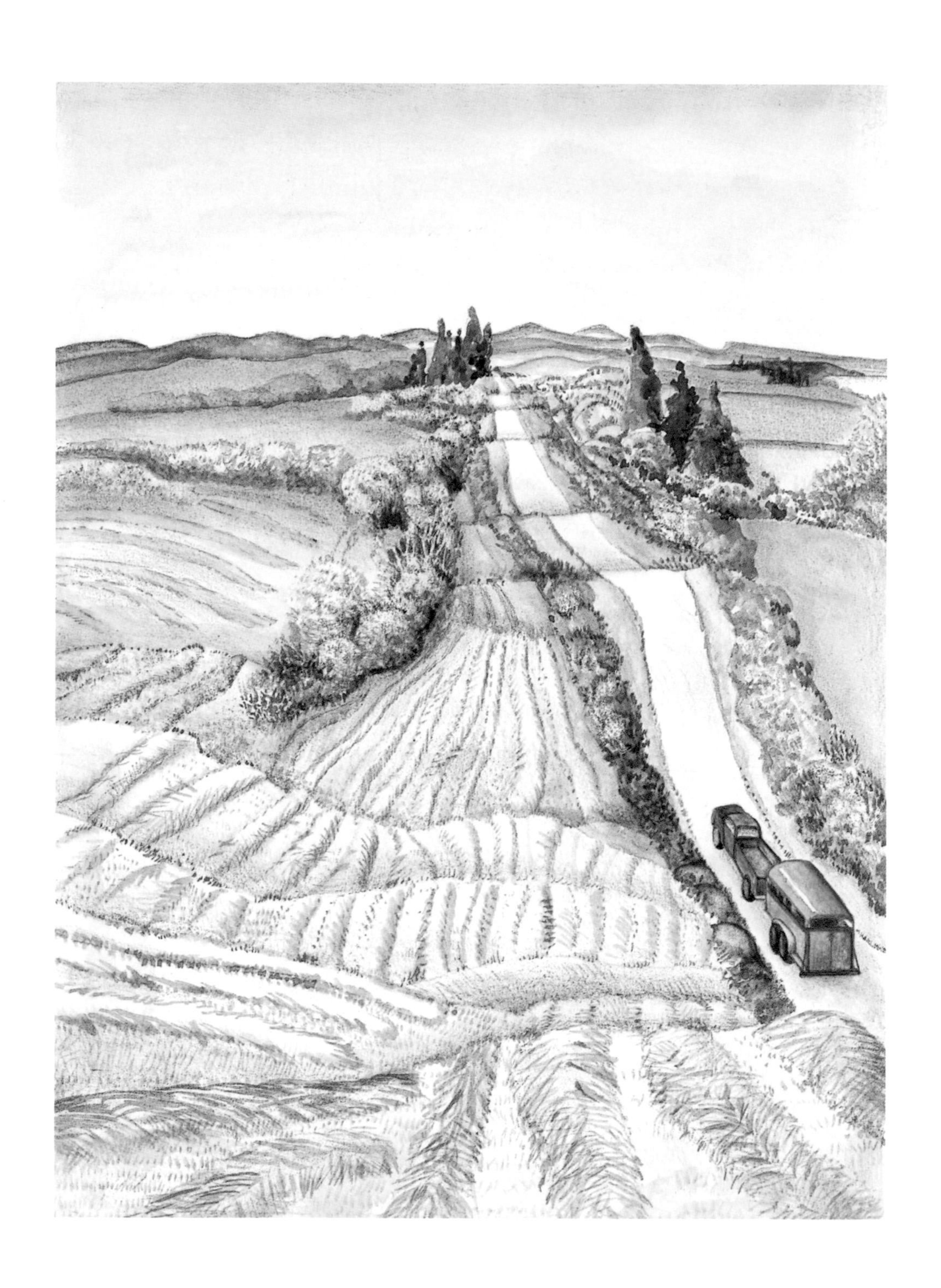

Jan spread fresh straw over the floor of the trailer so the calves would be cozy and warm. Then he and Victor led them to the ramp and carefully loaded them into the trailer. Jan climbed in with the animals and patted them gently.

"Come on, Jan! You can't ride back there," called Victor.

"All right," said Jan, climbing out and carefully closing the back of the trailer.

Jan and Victor drove home past fields full of wheat and barley almost ready for harvesting.

"You're driving too fast, Dad!" said Jan, thinking of the calves in the trailer behind them. "Do you think the brown-and-white calf could be mine?"

"If you look after it," Victor said.

They drove north for a while, then west. Giant combine machines kicked up dust as they rolled slowly over the fields. Then Victor pulled off the highway and followed the road up a hill.

They were home.

2 • Big Bear Farm

JAN ran into the house calling for his mother. He found her in the kitchen cooking dinner.

"So what have you brought home with you?" asked Barbara curiously.

Jan wasn't sure how to explain it.

"I think Father and I have done something crazy."

"What happened? Nothing bad?" asked Barbara.

"No, no, everything's okay. It's just that we bought seven Holstein calves because nobody else wanted them."

"Let me have a look," Barbara said, and they went out to the trailer.

"Oh!" she cried. "They're so sweet!"

Barbara patted the calves. "They're still very weak, the poor things. We have to feed them right away. But where are we going to get so much milk?"

She ran into the kitchen and looked through her list of phone numbers. Ernst and Stella ran a neighboring dairy farm with forty milk cows.

"Stella," Barbara cried into the telephone. "Victor and Jan have just brought home seven Holstein calves from the auction. They're only two weeks old. We'll need twenty-five liters of milk a day. When can I come?"

"You can come right away," Stella laughed. "I'll get everything ready."

Jan and Victor took the calves to the big barn. Jan spread fresh straw in the stalls, turned on the heat lamp and helped Victor move the animals.

The big breeding bull looked on. Henry, their Newfoundland farm dog, wagged his thick tail and barked. But by now the calves were too tired to take notice of anything.

Jan ran into the kitchen. His mother had already warmed the milk and filled seven bottles.

But when they took the bottles into the barn, none of the calves would take one. Barbara gently rubbed warm milk around one calf's muzzle and gave it one of her fingers to suck. Then she quickly stuck the nipple of the bottle into its mouth. The calf tasted the milk and began to suck slowly, then more and more quickly. Now one calf after another began to drink. Jan and Victor shoved the bottles into their mouths as fast as they could, and in no time the animals were a pushing, slurping muddle.

Jan gave each calf a name. He called the brown-and-white one Bruno. The smallest calf was named Tiny, and the biggest was called Magnus. The calves with the droopy ears and floppy skin were called Wrinkles and Flabby. The liveliest was Snowball, and the black one was called Slugger.

The next morning, Bruno and Tiny lay on the straw with sunken eyes and cold noses. Victor quickly carried them into the house and Barbara turned the bathroom into a sick bay.

Little Tiny died in the evening.

Now they all worried about Bruno. But during the second night they heard a loud "Mah!" When Jan looked in the bathroom, he saw Bruno standing up on four shaky legs.

Jan picked up the animal and immediately felt wet.

"What's going on?" he said, looking at Bruno more closely. "Oh, you're not a steer. You're a little girl calf. I'm going to call you...Anna!"

"My Anna! She's made it!" Jan ran to the kitchen, warmed milk and filled a bottle. Anna stood up and drank until it was empty.

"Tomorrow we'll take you back to the stall with the others," Jan murmured as he fell asleep.

During the next few days there was more bad luck. One morning Victor found the cow Galina lying dead in the pen behind the north barn. She had given birth to a calf ten days before. Victor couldn't figure out what had happened and only hoped that it was nothing contagious.

"Now we have another motherless little girl," he said, picking up the calf in his arms. "Come here, little Galina. I'm going to take you to Anna and the others so you won't be sad any more!"

The long summer holidays were over, and another school year began for Jan. In the morning he took the school bus into town. He saw wild geese flying south in their long rows. The swallows were flying away, too.

On the farm there was plenty to do before the winter. Threshing, baling, plowing. Victor and Barbara were glad that Jan was taking care of the calves after school. Anna mooed when she saw him coming with the milk. And little Galina was always beside her.

3 • A Long Winter

On Halloween the northwest wind pushed heavy clouds across the sky and blew the last leaves from the trees. The big herd came home for the winter from the grazed-off pastures. A late pair of ducks flew south, the lakes and ponds froze, and the ground became hard with frost.

One morning when he woke up, Jan saw that everything was white outside. His black cat, Muck, lay on the windowsill warming himself.

"Come outside," called Jan. "The snow is great!" But Muck didn't budge.

A few weeks later it began to snow heavily right at feeding time. The herd pushed into the barn without even touching the hay that was waiting in the round bale feeders. Fierce north winds drove fine snow into every cranny and blew wildly around the yard. Jan ran into the house, the ice stinging his face like needles. He was barely able to push the door closed.

"Looks like we're in for a blizzard!" he said as he pulled off his icy boots.

It stopped snowing just before noon the next day. The air became still and clear. The roads were closed and the school buses weren't running, so Jan could stay home and help.

The first thing Victor and Jan did was to shovel a path to the calf pen. It was hard work with the ice and snow, but thank goodness everything was all right in the barn. The water troughs hadn't frozen.

They fed the cows, and then the bigger animals came slowly out of the shed, white from head to hoof, their eyes and noses crusted with ice. This time they headed straight for the snow-covered hay in the feeders.

For a couple of hours the winter sun lit up the land. Then it sank to the purple horizon. After that it became bitterly cold. Victor had trouble starting the tractor, and it took him all day to clear away the mountains of snow. Jan froze miserably when he ran to the bus every morning. He was glad when the Christmas holidays finally came.

The days gradually became brighter, but winter still lasted a long time. Hungry birds swarmed around the feeders.

One extremely cold morning, the animals began to low reproachfully as soon as they saw Victor and Jan.

"Something's wrong," said Victor. Jan ran to the water troughs. They were frozen.

"We're going to get you something to drink!" he said to the herd. "But for now go out and lick the snow!" He and Victor got to work, but they forgot about the open gate. Too late, they saw the herd disappear around the corner, licking snow as they went.

"Hey, wait!" cried Victor, running after them so fast that he stumbled into a deep snowdrift.

When he finally came into the house, out of breath, he was in his stocking feet, holding an icy boot in each hand. He'd finally managed to round up the herd, but he was in bed with a cold for days after.

• • •

IT was time for the first calves to be born. The neighbors came and helped. Barbara and Jan fed and looked after the cows that were about to give birth. Usually calves came into the world and were patiently nursed by their mothers, but some just stood there dumbly at the beginning. Then you had to milk the cows and feed the calves with a bottle. But most were running around their mothers just a few hours after they were born. Anna and the big calves were long past this stage, but they got into the spirit of things anyway, romping and frisking about.

A warm southeast wind brought thaw, and gradually black earth appeared through the snow. Jan's rubber boots would get stuck in the mud when he went out to the barn to look after Anna and the calves.

When the sun came out, it became so warm that all the animals wheezed like steam engines, since they still had their thick winter coats. Water dripped from the eaves. Anna liked to catch it in her open mouth.

It was damp in the barn, too. Victor spread lots of straw around to keep things as dry and clean as possible, but calves still got sick, and two died that spring.

By Easter the wild ducks were swimming in the pond, frogs croaked day and night, and geese streamed north through the spring skies.

School was closed for the holiday, and Jan finally had time for Anna, little Galina and the young steers. They had all grown, and Jan was especially proud of Anna.

"You're getting horns!" he said as he patted her shiny coat. It had changed from dark brown to deep black over the past weeks. "Now you're a big girl!"

4 • Anna Grows Up

BEFORE long the meadows were green, and the animals were in high spirits. The dry, dusty remains of Victor's winter hay didn't taste good to them anymore, and they boldly stretched their necks over the fence of their pen. They were gradually losing their bristly winter coats.

It was time for the herd to go out to the grazing pasture by the beaver pond. Every year the neighbors helped. First the calves and cows were separated and vaccinated against diseases. Some received hoof treatments, and missing ear tags were replaced. Then they were loaded into the cattle trailer — first a load of calves, then a load of cows. The air would be filled with moos of protest until the animals were all happily reunited. Sometimes impatient cows would run back to the barnyard when they couldn't find their calves right away in the summer pasture.

The work went on until dark. Jan was tired, sunburnt and mosquito bitten, but he was happy and satisfied, too.

Out in the meadow the high grass rustled beneath the animals' bellies. They had trees to rub against, shady underbrush and a beaver pond full of water to drink.

Anna grazed with the other calves and a pair of old cows in the field behind the vegetable garden. She was still too young to be put out in the big pasture.

One day Barbara looked out the window.

"We have visitors," she cried. "Someone with a black-and-white cap just went by."

But no one came to the door. Only later did they find the visitors. Anna and her friends lay happily in Barbara's vegetable garden, right in the middle of the radish bed.

It was time to cut the hay. Victor sat in the mower for hours. The air smelled like peppermint and alfalfa. Now and then he saw porcupines, foxes, coyotes or hares fleeing the field, and he especially had to watch out for prairie hen nests. A neighbor helped him to bale the hay as soon as it was dry, and soon bales dotted the fields. The cattle would have plenty of winter feed this year.

But there had been no rain for a long time. The ground was hard and cracked. In the fields the corn was turning yellow far too early, and it had stopped growing. Mosquitoes and horseflies tormented Anna and the other animals. The sun shone mercilessly day after day.

At last a dark bank of clouds came. A hot wind whirled up dust and blew wildly through the trees. There was thunder and lightning, then fat drops of rain began to fall. It was as if a gray curtain was hanging from the sky. In the meadow the herd huddled together.

The storm marked the end of summer.

Thanksgiving fell on Jan's birthday this year. Barbara baked a special Thanksgiving-birthday meal. There were plenty of stories and lots of laughter. Everyone was happy. It had been a good year.

All the calves that had been born in the spring were now old enough to be weaned. Victor sold the bull calves and heifer calves that he didn't need.

When the snow began to fall, Anna became quieter. She was now almost full grown, so she and Galina were put with the big herd.

Over the next few months, Jan noticed that Anna was getting bigger and bigger.

"I think you're going to have a calf, Anna!" he said.

In the late spring Anna gave birth to her first calf, the black Anastasia. Anna was an excellent mother, and because she was a Holstein, she had so much milk that her calf was always the prettiest in the entire herd.

And that's how the Anna dynasty began at Big Bear Farm. Anna had a calf every year, as did Anastasia, and so Anna became great-great-grandmother to many, many cows. All of them had names beginning with A – Annabella, Amanda, Angelina, Afra, Agnes, Agatha, Amadea and Apollonia, just to name a few.

MANITOBA AGRICULTURE
CALVING RECORD BOOK
AGRICULTURE CANADA
MANITOBA LIVESTOCK PERFORMANCE TESTING BOARD INC.
CALVING RECORD BOOK
1997 CALVING RECORD
Calf ID
Name of calf
Sex
Sire
Birth DATE D M
Birth Wt.
1 Schnurrbärtle f Prince 2 7 85
1 Weisse f 3 7 80
2 Doubleface m 4 7 95
3 Carol m 5 7 70
4 Carol m Leo 6 7 110
5 Amadea f 6 7 90
6 Pünktchen m 6 7 95
7 Jessi f
G RECORD
calving remarks
informations
buckskin white f.
tanned shinny
buckskin white face
easy pull
hell lockig
buckskin white f.
brown f.
breech
brown eyes white f.
1995 CALVING RECORD
1 Betsy f
2 Angelina f
3 Doofe m
4 Palma f
5 Bessi m
6 Uschi f
7 Marla
1991 CALVING RECORD
Leo
1 Shorty f
2 Afra f
3 Geissgeiss
4 18erl
5 Linchen
Herford d.f.
white face
buckskin w.f.
white
buckskin
brown black nose
white dot
dotted f.
calving remarks
info
Herford
brown
tan w.f.
simmental
Herford
brown eyes
black
dotted f.
buckskin
white f.
brown eyes
simmental
7 Anastasia f 14 4 75
8 Jan m 17 4 95
9 Tüpferl m 18 4 100
10 Bless m 19 4 95
11 25erl
pull
1987 CALVING RECORD
Calf I.D.
Name of calf
Sex
Sire
BIRTH DATE D M
H or P
Birth Wt.
Calving remarks
Notice
01 Leni f Prince 7 4 75
02 Agatha f Duke 7 4 100
03 Zenzi f 8 4 90
04 Muckerle m 9 4 95
05 Carla f 9 4 100
06 Pimpernel m 10 4 80
07 Bicca f 13 4 95
08 Gunda f 14 4 95
09 Jora m 16 4 100
09 Plüschohr Prince 17 4 75
10 Mitzi f 17 4 95
11
simmental tan
black sprinkled face
pull brown, white
buckskin
tan, w.f.
e. pull
geschecken
dark, wh
tamed
brown
1988 CALVING RECORD
Calving remarks
Info.
1 Fabian Judy f Emil 18 4 100
2 Woleshen 19 4 85
3 Mandy m 23 4 90
4 Agnes f 24 4 97
5 Ulla f 25 4 95
6 Jessica f 4 5 120
7 Miller m 6 5 110
8 Mama 22 5 100
9 Rothörnle 25 5 75
10 Daisy 25 5 95
dark eyes white f.
easy pull
brown
dotted face
white grey
breech
buckskin uni
white pink nose
buckskin dotted
white face
pull
tan white
gestreift, beige